For Charlie James
C. H.
For Vijay, Sashi, and Ravinder
J. H.

FIRST EDITION

1 3 5 7 9 10 8 6 4 2

Library of Congress Catalog Card Number: 92–72025
ISBN: 1–56282–342–6/1–56282–343–4 (lib. bdg.)

Stormy Day

Claire Henley

Hyperion Books For Children
New York

Huge black clouds gather.
The sky looks cold and dark.
There will be stormy weather today.

The wind howls and moans.
It swoops down and blows leaves off trees
and hats off heads.

Far away bright lightning flashes.
Thunder booms and rumbles all around.
Timmy barks and barks.

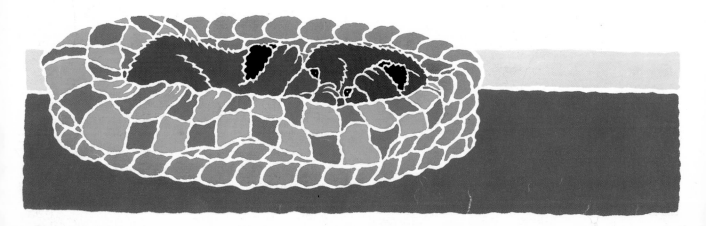

Drops of rain begin to fall.
Pitter-patter, pitter-patter on the ground.
A tiny mouse scurries back to its hole.

Raindrops drip off the trees.
They land in big shiny puddles –
splish, splash.

Down come the hailstones,
drumming on the roof.
They crash against the walls
and bounce on the path.
Quick! Close the windows,
shut the doors!

Ginger and her kittens scamper inside
just in time.
They don't like their paws getting wet.

Some animals don't mind the rain.
On the lake swans swim happily.
Ducks bob up and down on the waves.

Glistening green frogs like
damp places and rainy skies.
The spider hurries to find shelter
at the edge of its web.

We have big striped umbrellas to hide under.
Sometimes it's fun to play in the rain.

We have yellow raincoats and
red boots to keep us dry.
We run and race and
jump in the puddles.
Look out! Here we come!

Look! There's a rainbow.
Soon the storm will be over,
and the sun will shine.

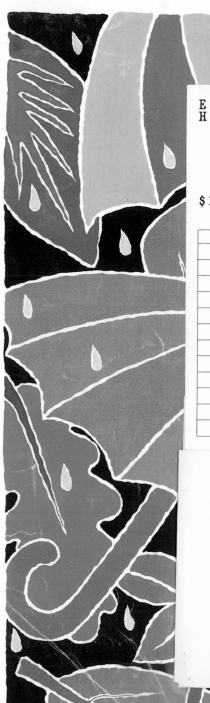

DATE			